The Best Christmas Ever!

Marni McGee

Gavin Scott

LITTLE TIGER PRESS

London

Millicent Mouse was **all a-flutter!**
Christmas was only one day away,
and the little mouse could hardly wait.

She had swept and scrubbed until everything sparkled. She had fluffed and dusted until she sneezed.

Millicent gathered
apples and nuts from
the cellar.

In a flurry of
flour, she baked
an apple-nut pie.

She poured honey and spices into a kettle. Standing on tiptoe, she sniffed – and smiled.

"Christmas just **wouldn't** be Christmas," she said, "without my hot honey punch and apple-nut pie."

Millicent bundled up warm,
then scampered out into the snow.
Her black boots crunched as
she walked to and fro, gathering
lots and lots of ivy.

"Christmas just **wouldn't** be Christmas," she puffed, "**without** fresh ivy for my wreath and berries to string on my tree."

But instead of berries, Millicent found a baby hedgehog, snoring softly in the snow. **"Witchety whiskers!"** she gasped and tiptoed close. "He needs a better nest than that!"

So she wove all of her ivy into a leafy
blanket and gently tucked it around him.

By the time Millicent had finished, the sky was growing dark. "**Fiddle!**" she fussed. "Too late to search for berries now."

Millicent scurried home.

There she found Felicity Finch and her chicks, searching for food.

"**What-oh-what** shall we do?" the mother bird cried. "The snow has covered our seeds."

"Come in where it's warm," said Millicent. "I've just made an apple-nut pie."

In the flick of a wing, the kitchen was full
of hungry chicks. Their feathers fluttered and
flapped as they flocked around Millicent's pie.

Millicent heard a knock at the door. "**Fiddle!**" she muttered. "Whatever **now?**"

"Berry Chribbas, Billicent," called Gabriel Skunk. "I brogg you a bresent. Berfume."

"**Perfume!**" said Millicent, hiding a smile. "**Why, thank you.**" Gabriel dabbed at his nose. "I hab a tebbible code."

"Try my hot honey punch," she said. "It's very good for a terrible cold."

Gabriel lifted the kettle and drank every drop.

"Thaggs," he said and ambled off home.

Millicent looked all around. "It looks as if **a storm** has hit! Every dish is **dirty**. My pie and my punch are gobbled and **gone**. I have **no** ivy for my wreath, **no** berries for my tree. **Witchety whiskers!**

HOW can Christmas be Christmas NOW?"

Then Millicent smiled. "At least I have my berfume…Perfume from a skunk!" she giggled, and bustled off to bed. "The baby hedgehog is **warm**," she whispered. "The chicks are **full** of pie, and the punch will **help** dear Gabriel's cold."

And with a yawn she fell asleep.

The next morning, Millicent woke to a chorus of cheeps and chirps. Outside were robins, sparrows and finches, and they were all singing – for her!

Behind the birds came a family of hedgehogs.
Grandfather Hedgehog carried a sack, and the
baby had flowers stuck in his prickly spines.

Cheepy-cheep!

Chirp!

Cheepy-cheep!

Last came Gabriel Skunk – with a
lopsided grin and a great big cake!
"Gracious goodness!"
exclaimed Millicent. She invited them in.

They trimmed the tree together with treasures
from Grandfather Hedgehog's sack – buttons
and ribbons, sparkling foil,
and scraps of cloth.

Millicent's black eyes sparkled. "This is the very **best Christmas ever!** And I am surely the happiest mouse in the forest. Christmas just couldn't be Christmas without my **wonderful friends!"**